HOPSCOTCH FAIRY TALES

The Princess and the Pea

Retold by Anne Walter

Illustrated by Jane Cope

W

FRANKLIN WATTS

LONDON • SYDNEY

First published in 2009 by
Franklin Watts
338 Euston Road
London
NW1 3BH

Franklin Watts Australia
Level 17/207 Kent Street
Sydney
NSW 2000

A CIP catalogue record for this book is available
from the British Library.

ISBN 978 0 7496 8541 6 (hbk)
ISBN 978 0 7496 8547 8 (pbk)

Series Editor: Melanie Palmer
Series Advisor: Dr Barrie Wade
Series Designer: Peter Scoulding

Printed in China

Franklin Watts is a division of
Hachette Children's Books,
an Hachette UK company
www.hachette.co.uk

Once upon a time there was

a handsome prince.

He had nearly everything
he could ever want:

a palace,

a horse,

and plenty
of gold.

4

But he was missing one thing –
a princess! A *real* princess was
very hard to find.

The king and queen wanted
the prince to get married.
They decided to help so they
sent posters to every town.

Soon crowds of girls came to
the palace. Everyone wanted
to marry the prince!

There were so many girls that the
guards had to lock the palace
gates. But the girls kept coming.

The prince saw every kind of girl,
from every country and every town.
They all tried to be a princess – but
none of them was a *real* princess!

"Oh dear!" sighed the prince.
"How will I ever find my
princess?" He went to bed
feeling very sad.

11

In the middle of the night, there was a terrible storm. Lightning flashed and thunder crashed. Rain poured and poured.

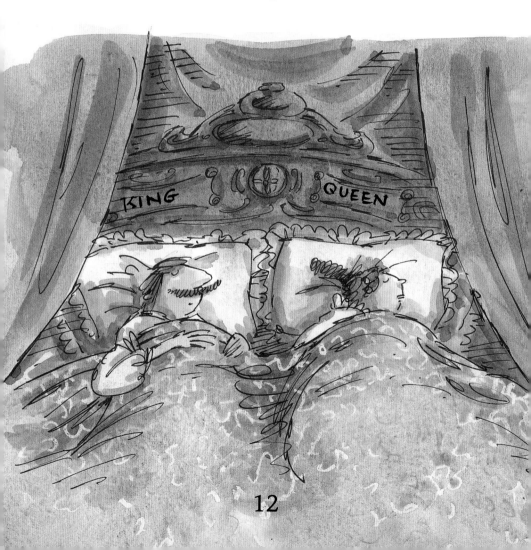

Suddenly there was a noise
outside the palace gates.
"Let me in, let me in,"
cried a little voice.

The voice woke up the king.

"Who can that be?" he thought.

So he went to see.

"Please help me, I'm lost. Can I come in?" called the little voice. The king opened up the gates.

There stood a girl covered in mud.
She was wet from head to toe.
"I'm a princess," she said,
"and I've lost my way."

The king was surprised.

"You don't look like a *real*

princess," he thought.

The queen was shocked.

"What a messy girl you are!"

she said. "You'd better have a bath

and then go straight to bed!"

"I wonder if she is a *real* princess,"
thought the queen. Then she
thought of a plan to test her.
"I shall put this pea in her bed.

Then I will put twenty mattresses
on top of it. Only a *real* princess
will be able to feel the pea
underneath them."

The princess was very sleepy as
she climbed into bed, on top
of the twenty mattresses.

But she didn't sleep a wink all
night. She could feel something
in her bed.

Next morning, the queen saw the
princess and asked, "How did you
sleep, young lady?"

"Not well at all," replied the
princess, yawning. "There was
something bumpy in my bed."

"Wonderful!" said the king
"Marvellous!" said the queen.
"I've found a *real* princess!"
cheered the prince. "Will you
marry me?" he asked.
"Yes!" said the princess.

Next day there was a royal
wedding. Many people came
to the palace, but there was
only one *real* princess.

Puzzle 1

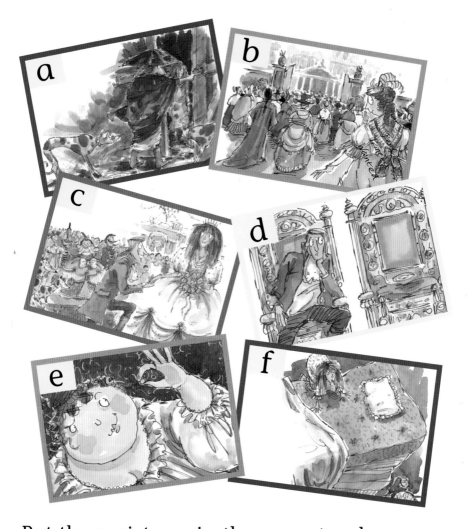

Put these pictures in the correct order.

Which event do you think is most important?

Now try writing the story in your own words!

Puzzle 2

Choose the correct speech bubbles for each character. Can you think of any others? Turn over to find the answers.

Answers

Puzzle 1

The correct order is 1d, 2b, 3a, 4e, 5f, 6c.

Puzzle 2

The prince: 2, 6

The queen: 1, 4

The princess: 3, 5